For Joe and Leo,
sweet dreams always—J.D.

To my father, Dudley Reynolds, who first told me
about the Imperial Elephant, and to his grandchildren
and great-grandchildren, because he would want
them to know this story too—D.R.R.

Text copyright © 2003 by Diana Reynolds Roome
Pictures copyright © 2003 by Jude Daly
By arrangement with The Inkman, Cape Town, South Africa
Printed and bound in Singapore
First published in Great Britain, in somewhat different form, by Frances Lincoln Limited, 2003
First American edition, 2003
1 3 5 7 9 10 8 6 4 2

Library of Congress Cataloging-in-Publication Data
Roome, Diana Reynolds.
The elephant's pillow / Diana Reynolds Roome ; pictures by Jude Daly.— 1st
American ed.
p.   cm.
Summary: Sing Lo, a wealthy boy living in Peking, goes to visit the late emperor's
Imperial Elephant and tries to cheer him up.
ISBN 0-374-32015-2
[1. Elephants—Fiction.   2. Beijing (China)—Fiction.   3. China—Fiction.]
I. Daly, Jude, ill.   II. Title.

PZ7.R67214 El 2003
[E]—dc21
2002192544

THE ELEPHANT'S PILLOW

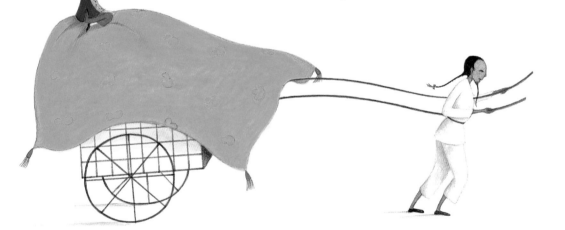

Diana Reynolds Roome

Pictures by Jude Daly

FARRAR, STRAUS AND GIROUX
NEW YORK

L ong ago in the city of Peking,
there lived a boy named
Sing Lo.

His father was a rich merchant,
so he had everything he could want.

One morning Li, his rickshaw man,
arrived to take him for an outing.
Li knew every paving stone of Peking
and had shown Sing Lo all the grand
sights. But Sing Lo wasn't satisfied.

"What is the greatest sight of all?"
he asked.

"Once, when I was little," said Li, panting as he ran,
"my father took me to see a royal parade. The Emperor
passed right by us on his elephant!"

"I wish to see this Imperial Elephant," demanded Sing Lo.

"When the old Emperor died," Li said sadly, "the elephant refused to carry anyone. People say that now he is a nasty-tempered beast."

Sing Lo thought hard.

"Maybe a present would cheer him up," he suggested.

"I've heard," said Li, "that the old Emperor used to give him special buns.
Let's visit my friend Wang Ching, the best baker in all Peking."

Off they sped to Bakers Street. They stopped at a stall selling nothing but buns,
glazed with honey and sprinkled with poppy seeds.

"How many?" asked Wang Ching.

"All you have," said Li. "The Imperial Elephant has waited a long time."

At last they arrived at a temple. A priest came out to greet them.

"I've come to see the Imperial Elephant," announced Sing Lo.

The priest looked worried.

"The elephant doesn't like visitors," he said. But he led Sing Lo
to a great, dark door covered with metal studs. From behind the door
came snuffling sounds. The ground shook a little as something
enormous stomped about inside.

"Be careful," muttered the priest. "Ever since
the old Emperor died, the elephant hasn't slept a wink."
He pulled open the door and walked quickly away.

Inside, in the dim light, Sing Lo could see a huge shape.

"O Imperial Elephant," called Sing Lo nervously. "I have something for you."

The elephant did not move.

Sing Lo rustled the paper bag. He stared as one beady eye opened and one leathery ear twitched.

"Your favorites," said Sing Lo, edging away.

Slowly the great gray trunk unfurled. One bun disappeared, then another . . . and another . . . until not a poppy seed was left.

But the elephant stood shifting back and forth uneasily.

Sing Lo thought hard. "If I had just eaten a huge bag of buns, what would I want?"

There was a low, rumbly sound as the elephant touched Sing Lo's ear.

A drink! Of course. But what kind of drink?

"Wait here," said Sing Lo.

Outside, the priest was waiting under a ginkgo tree.

"The elephant needs a bedtime drink," declared Sing Lo.

The priest looked surprised, but he bowed and walked back to the temple. Soon he came out holding an empty golden bowl.

"Honey above, ginger below, milk between," the priest said solemnly.

"What can he mean?" thought Sing Lo. He took the bowl and hurried back to the rickshaw. Li would know what to do. But Li was fast asleep. Sing Lo prodded him and tugged his pigtail, but Li would not wake up.

"I'll have to get it myself," said Sing Lo rather crossly. He'd never had to do much of anything for himself before now.

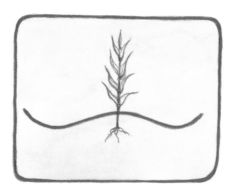

He gazed up at the
ginkgo tree. Among the
leaves, he caught sight
of a wild bees' nest.

"Honey above!" he
exclaimed. He inched
up the trunk and
pulled off a sticky
chunk of honeycomb.
But an angry bee
followed him down.

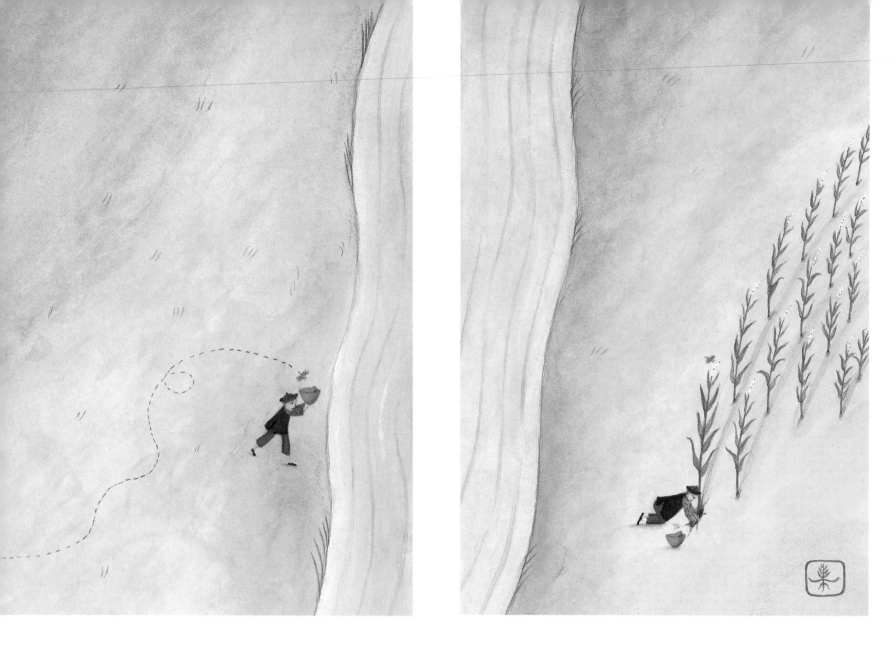

Sing Lo dashed toward the river, holding the bowl and the honey high.
As he pulled himself out of the water, he sniffed a delicious fragrance—
and there was the bee gathering ginger-blossom nectar.

"Ginger below!" he cried, and dug down to pull up a ginger root.

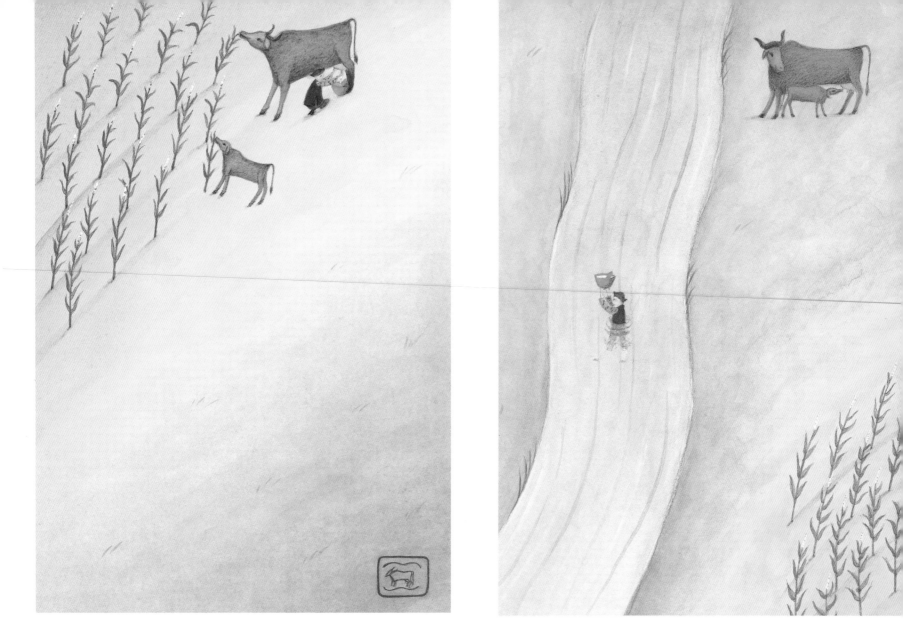

Munching contentedly on the patch of plants stood a buffalo and her calf.

"Milk between!" whispered Sing Lo triumphantly, and the buffalo hardly noticed when he helped himself. With honey, ginger, and milk in the bowl, he waded back across the river.

Outside the elephant's stall, Sing Lo
stirred the drink. He pulled open
the great door and held out the bowl.

The elephant plopped in his trunk
and sucked—*thhssswpp!* He swung
his trunk up under his chin and shot
the drink into his mouth. Not a drop
was spilled.

But instead of lying down to sleep,
the elephant swung his trunk, almost
knocking Sing Lo off his feet.

What was bothering him? Sing Lo
looked around. Of course! A pile of
dirty straw was hardly a suitable bed
for an Imperial Elephant.

"I'll be back," said Sing Lo quietly.

He dashed out to the rickshaw.

"Li," he said. "Take me to Silk Street!" He explained what he needed.

"My friend Ab Fat is the best silk merchant in all Peking," Li replied.

"Master could visit him tomorrow."

"The Imperial Elephant cannot wait," said Sing Lo. "Hurry!"

"Good day, Ab Fat," said Li, skidding to a stop. "My master needs
a yellow pillow—this big—with tassels. Have it ready by this afternoon."

When they arrived back at the temple, the sun was low in the sky.
From inside came the mysterious sounds of chanting.

"Close your eyes tightly," Sing Lo whispered to the elephant as he dragged the pillow into the stall. He arranged the pillow on top of the straw.

"Behold, O Imperial Elephant!" he cried.

The elephant opened one eye and stared at the pillow. He felt it carefully with his trunk.

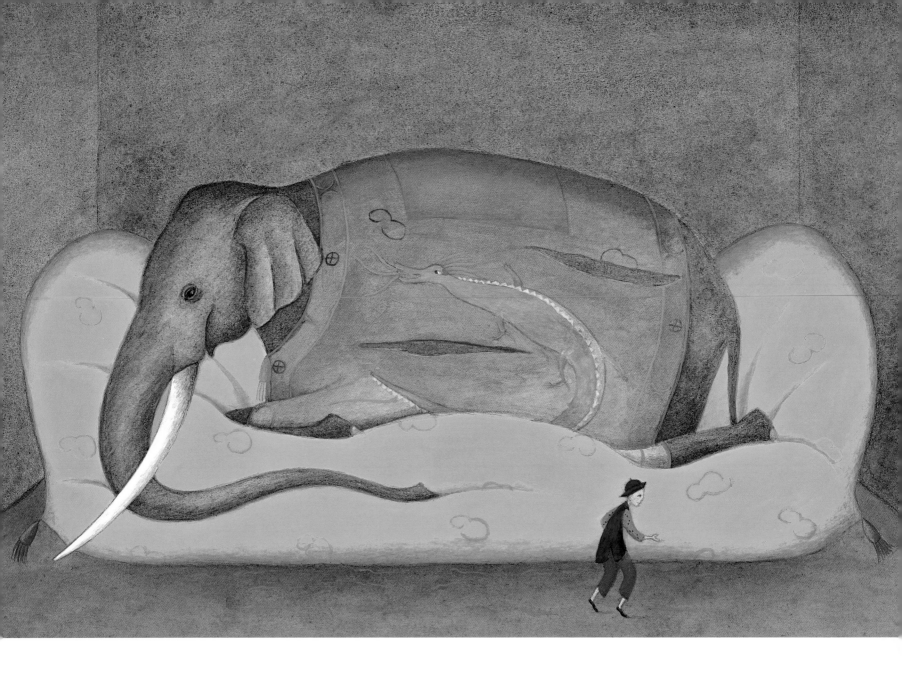

His back knees bent, his front knees folded. With a huge sigh, his head sank down.

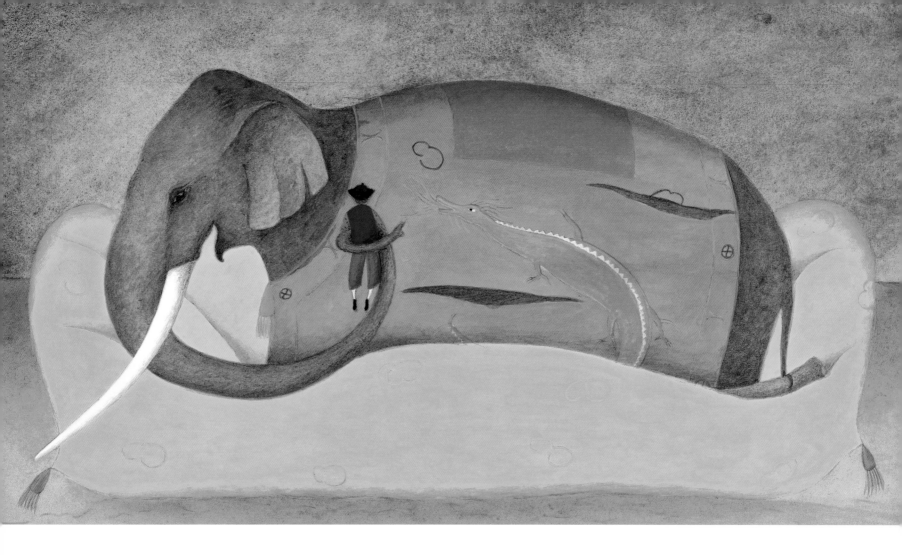

    Suddenly the elephant stretched out his trunk and curled it
gently around the boy.

    Sing Lo gasped as he felt himself lifted up . . . up . . . and onto
the elephant's back. There was a rumble as the elephant nudged
Sing Lo up, until he was sitting just behind his ear.

    Then the great trunk tapped Sing Lo's hand.

    "What now?" asked Sing Lo. But somehow he knew.

He stretched out his hand to scratch . . . scratch . . . scratch . . . the gnarled neck.

Slowly the elephant's head started to sink down until it touched the pillow. His eyes closed, and his head sank deeper into the soft yellow silk. Soon a low thrum of snoring joined the chanting from the temple.

Sing Lo smiled.

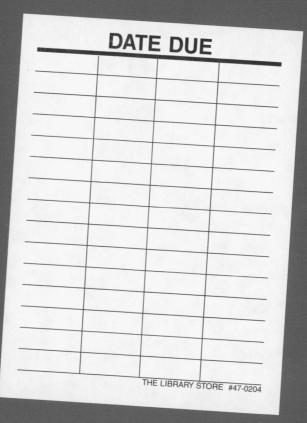